I HAVE AN OLIVE TREE

by EVE BUNTING   illustrated by KAREN BARBOUR

JOANNA COTLER BOOKS

An Imprint of HarperCollins *Publishers*

To Alex Uhl and to Nancy Kellogg,
who brought us together
—E.B.

To Joan and Sumner
—K.B.

I Have an Olive Tree
Text copyright © 1999 by Edward D. Bunting and Anne E. Bunting,
trustees of the Edward D. Bunting and Anne E. Bunting Family Trust
Illustrations copyright © 1999 by Karen Barbour
Manufactured in China. All rights reserved.
http://www.harperchildrens.com

Library of Congress Cataloging-in-Publication Data
Bunting, Eve, 1928–
    I have an olive tree / Eve Bunting ; illustrated by Karen Barbour.
        p.   cm.
    "Joanna Cotler books."
    Summary: After her grandfather's death, eight-year-old Sophia fulfills
his last request and journeys to Greece with her mother to see the land
where her roots are.
    ISBN 0-06-027573-1. — ISBN 0-06-027574-X (lib. bdg.)
    1. Greek Americans—Juvenile fiction.   [1. Greek Americans—
Fiction.   2. Greece—Fiction.]   1. Barbour, Karen, ill.   II. Title.
PZ7.B91527Iaar   1999   98-7213
[E]—dc21   CIP
                                                                        AC

7 8 9 10
❖

The day I was seven, my grandfather gave me an olive tree.

"Happy birthday, Sophia," he said.

"Where's the tree?" my brother Georgios asked.

"It is in Greece. On the island," Grandfather said.

We all know about Greece and the island where my grandparents lived before they came to California. The island where my mother was born.

"When we left the island, we sold everything," my grandfather explained. "But the new owners let us keep the tree. It was a symbol."

"What does *that* mean?" Georgios asked.

"The olive tree was something of ours that was rooted in Greek earth," Grandfather said. "It is in the field behind the house that was ours. Now, Sophia, I give it to you."

Grandfather kissed me and I smiled, but I didn't really understand.

"Your grandmother used to climb into that tree and pick olives and let them fall into a net below," Grandfather said. "She was a wonderful picker."

Mama gave him a hug. "She had to be. She picked you."

Grandfather nodded. He took Grandmother's string of beads from his pocket and let them trickle through his fingers. Grandfather carried them always since the time she died.

"Thank you for the tree, Grandfather," I said.

"Sophia really wanted a skateboard," Georgios told him.

"Be quiet, Georgios," Papa warned.

I had wanted a skateboard, and I didn't want an olive tree. What would I do with it?

My grandfather died a year after he gave me the tree. We were all with him around his bed. Mama had brought him Grandmother's beads to hold, and he crumpled them up and gave them to me. At first I thought he wanted me to have them for a keepsake. But he said, "Sophia? Will you go to the island and hang these in your olive tree, for Grandmother and me? I have asked your mother if she will take you, and she has agreed."

I was all puddled up and sniffly. I nodded, but I wasn't sure how Mama and I could do this. Later Mama told me how Grandfather had been saving and saving. "The money is so we can go to Greece, Sophia," she said.

Mama and I took a plane to Athens and then a cab to the docks. Everything looked different. It was strange to think we had come so far from home. Mama got quieter and quieter. Sometimes she read aloud the names written in Greek above the shops as if she liked the sound of them in her mouth.

The woman who sold tickets to ride the ferry spoke some English.
"There is only one boat a day," she told us. "It is just a small island."

"I know," Mama said.

The woman eyed Mama's suitcase and my backpack. "You will be staying at the house and board of Alexandra Grammos?"

"Yes," Mama said. "For two nights only. It has been arranged."

We sat on a wooden bench to wait. People bustled around us and talked in Greek. Some of them carried baskets almost as big as themselves. Ferryboats came and left. Never ours. A sponge seller, his sponges stacked around him like great lumps of honeycomb, called out his prices. I wanted to get one for me and one for Georgios, but Mama said no. Maybe on the way back.

Mama shook me awake when the ferry came. As soon as I opened my eyes, I thought, *I'm in Greece.* But it didn't seem real.

There was a priest on the ferry with us. He had on a long black robe and his hair was pinned up in a bun under his hat. There was also a woman with a flock of sheep. They baaed and bleated and to me they seemed to be speaking American sheep talk, not Greek. The woman let me pet them.

"There is good grazing on the island," Mama said, but even as she spoke she leaned across the side of the boat, not looking at me, or the priest, or the sheep woman, or the sheep. I held on to the back of her jacket. She seemed to be reaching across the sea. It was as if she was ready to fly.

"There it is!" she whispered. Her finger shook as she pointed, and I saw a misty hump sticking out of the water. The priest smiled and said something in Greek, and after a minute Mama smiled at him and nodded.

"What did he say?"

"I think he asked if we were going home."

"But we're not," I said.

Before we got to the dock we could hear music, like a guitar, and as we edged into the mooring we saw a man with a droopy mustache sitting on a box.

"That's a bouzouki he's playing," Mama said.

The priest waved us ahead of him and then we all had to jump quickly to the side as the sheep came stampeding down the little gangplank.

"We'll go to the olive tree first," Mama said.

"But we'll have to carry the suitcase. And my backpack." The backpack had been getting heavier and heavier ever since we left home.

"The tree's not far," Mama said. "Nothing is far on this island."

We walked past houses, whitewashed, sleeping in the sun. Sometimes my mother stopped and put the suitcase down and I thought she was resting, but I could see she was looking at things and probably remembering.

A woman carrying a bucket came out of a house. She called out to us in Greek.

"What did she say?" I asked.

"It sounded like 'Have a nice day!'" Mama smiled.

The road narrowed. Rock roses climbed the hedges.

"Look at the sky," Mama said. "It's blue light."

I was feeling something strange. My chest hurt. I began to cry.

"It's all right." Mama drew a shaky, noisy breath. "There's the house we lived in, Sophia. There's the field."

We walked across the field, the suitcase between us bumping our legs, the straps of the backpack cutting into my neck.

Two goats cropped the grass. A bigger one drank from a rusty bathtub. Another looked as if it might run at us, and I got behind Mama. But the goat didn't move.

"There's your tree," Mama said.

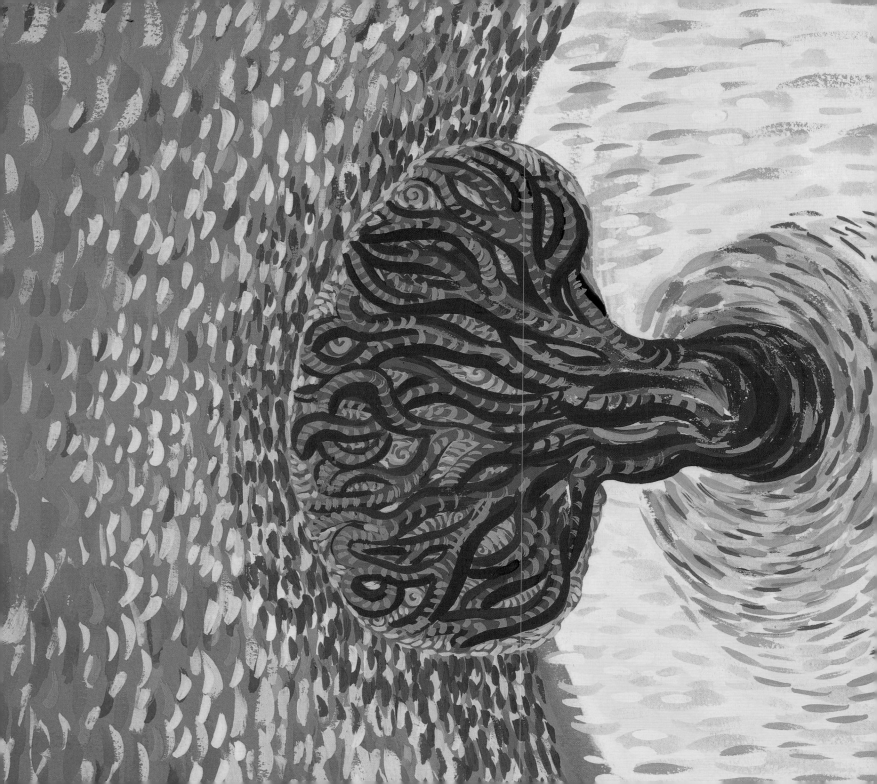

It was not the way I had imagined.

We stood beneath it.

"No olives," Mama said. "I expect it's too old."

I put my hand on the trunk. It was dry and rough and knotted.

Mama gave me a tissue so I could wipe my eyes and blow my nose.

"Should I get the beads now?" I asked.

She nodded.

My fingers were fumbly as I unbuckled the backpack, took out the beads, and let them stream into my hand. "Look how the sun traps itself in them."

"They are like liquid gold," Mama said.

"They are like big bubbles of honey," I said. I gave them to Mama.

"I can't reach."

"Grandfather wanted you to do it." She lifted me, and I hung the beads high on a branch.

I watched the beads glitter in the sunlight, and then I pulled the tree's leaves around to hide them. Grandfather would be pleased, I thought, and I knew that this wasn't the only reason Grandfather had wanted us to come. It had to do with Mama and me and all of us being part of the island. He wanted Mama to remember again, and he wanted me to know. I did know. I'd never forget the island. Someday I'd come back.

I tugged at Mama's hand.

"I have an olive tree," I said.